WHICH WAY BOOKS #15

STAR TREK:® VOYAGE TO ADVENTURE

Michael J. Dodge

ILLUSTRATED BY GORDON TOMEI

AN ARCHWAY PAPERBACK
Published by POCKET BOOKS • NEW YORK

Attention!

Which Way Books must be read in a special way. DO NOT READ THE PAGES IN ORDER. If you do, the story will make no sense at all. Instead, follow the directions at the bottom of each page until you come to an ending. Only then should you return to the beginning and start over again, making different choices this time.

There are many possibilities for exciting adventures. Some of the endings are good; some of the endings are bad. If you meet a terrible fate, you can reverse it in your next story by making new choices.

Remember: follow the directions carefully, and have fun!

You are an Ensign in Starfleet, just graduated from the Starfleet Academy. Because of your high scores as a cadet, you have been assigned to the starship *Enterprise,* commanded by Captain James T. Kirk.

As you pick up your space bag and prepare to beam aboard the *Enterprise,* you can remember the speech Admiral Traynor gave to your class of Ensigns. . . .

"Never forget that Starfleet's mission is to keep peace in the galaxy. Use force only when everything else has failed.

"And never forget the Prime Directive: Do not interfere with an alien race, even if you think you would be doing the right thing. We do not always understand the ways of other peoples, and sometimes our 'help' may only make things worse. Power is a terrible thing unless it is used wisely.

"Now, best of luck to all of you."

The transporter operator pushes the controls, and light surrounds you. You are beamed aboard the *Enterprise*.

Turn to page 2.

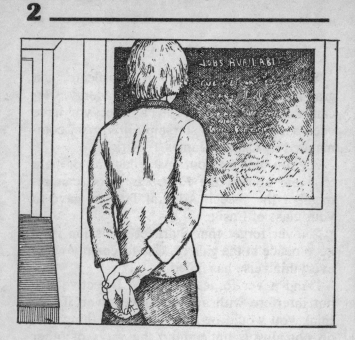

It is time to choose your assignment aboard the *Enterprise*. There is a board that shows the jobs available, but it does not say very much about them.

If you want to try Engineering, go to page 3.

If you choose to work on the Bridge, go to page 4.

If you prefer a job in the Science Laboratory, go to page 5.

You get out of the turbo-lift on the ship's Engineering deck. Ahead of you are the enormous warp engines that power the *Enterprise*. To one side, you can see Chief Engineer Scott working at a control panel. As you start toward Mr. Scott, a tall man in a Lieutenant's uniform steps into your path.

"Another new Ensign?" he says, sounding annoyed. "Well, I'm Lieutenant Grogan, and I know what to do with you." He hands you an electronic sweeper. "Take this and get to work cleaning the deck."

If you agree to obey Lieutenant Grogan and start sweeping, go to page 6.

If you want to complain to Mr. Scott that you are an Ensign, not a janitor, go to page 24.

You arrive on the Bridge. On the display screen ahead, stars are flashing past. As you step from the turbo-lift, Captain Kirk turns to face you.

"Welcome aboard, Ensign," the Captain says. "We've been receiving some strange transmissions from an uncharted planet in this sector. Your job will be to help Lieutenant Uhura translate and list them."

You take a seat next to Lieutenant Uhura. She smiles and points to a huge pile of tape cassettes on one side of the console, and a pair of headphones on the other. "There's a lot of work to do," she says. "Where do you want to start?"

If you wish to use the translating computer on the recordings already made, go to page 50.

If you prefer listening to the transmissions through the headphones, go to page 43.

You enter the ship's Science Laboratory. The walls are lined with crystal panels in rainbow colors, glowing with light. At the center of the room, Science Officer Spock is working at a computer console unlike any you have ever seen before.

Mr. Spock turns to face you. "Good day, Ensign. We are now in a part of space where the flow of time is twisted back on itself. I have constructed this device to analyze the time flow. Please help me adjust the crystal control frames."

You take a step forward. Suddenly one of the crystal panels cracks and shatters. Colored light sprays across the room and over Mr. Spock.

"Stay out of the time field!" Spock orders. "Do not touch me!"

If you obey Mr. Spock, turn to page 82.

If you try to pull Spock out of the field despite his orders, turn to page 86.

Lieutenant Grogan nods his head as you take the sweeper and go to work.

Because of the electronic sweeper, cleaning the deck is not hard work, but it is very dull. As you sweep a corner, behind some machinery you see something small and shiny and very fast move across the floor in front of you.

Curious, you follow the shiny streak. Soon it disappears into what looks like a solid wall. But when you tap the wall, you find that a panel is loose, and behind it is a tunnel just big enough for you to enter.

You do not see anyone else around. You go into the tunnel. The only light comes from the little headlight on your electronic sweeper. You can hear the hum of the ship's main power lines all around you. On the floor are little bits of metal and plastic, and you follow their trail.

After many twists and turns, you come to a small room. In the corners are piles of sparkling metal: electronic parts. In the middle of the floor is something that looks like a large mouse, but made of metal—a robot! It looks up at you with red, electric eyes.

If you decide to hit at the "mouse," turn to page 21.

If you want to hold still and see what the robot does, go to page 10.

You push the controls hard to portside. The planet swings past the ship: The *Enterprise* trembles as it scrapes the planet's atmosphere.

"There's structural damage, sir," you hear Mr. Scott say from the Engineering console.

"Not so close next time, Ensign," says Captain Kirk.

Another Klingon disruptor shot flashes past the *Enterprise*. You are in a tight orbit around the planet, the Klingon warship just behind you.

Then, just ahead, you see two more Klingon ships waiting for you.

"Warp speed *now*, Helmsman," the Captain orders.

Mr. Scott says, "The engines are damaged, Captain. I can't give you warp power for twenty seconds yet."

Kirk says, "Scotty, we may not be here in twenty seconds. Any ideas, Helmsman?"

If you try to turn the Enterprise *and run for deep space, away from the planet, turn to page 78.*

If you want to fly the ship directly between the Klingon cruisers, trying to surprise them, turn to page 80.

You use your tricorder's sensors to scan the blob. You discover that it is a living creature, and it seems to be eating pure energy from the power cables in the wall of the Jeffries tube.

As you watch, the energy-creature shakes like a bowl of pudding. And it becomes larger, until it is half as big as you are. If it grows as much with the next shake, it will be bigger than you.

If you decide to kill the lump, go to page 79.

If you would rather get the creature out of the ship, go to page 25.

You begin to climb the ladder up the Jeffries tube, toward the point of energy far above.

As you get nearer the point, the red OVER-LOAD light on your tricorder starts flashing. Then the sensor goes dead. Sparks crackle around the metal parts of your radiation suit as you continue to climb.

Finally, you see that the center of the electric storm is a metal box on the wall of the tube. You can tell that the box is some kind of computer, one of the small ones that controls the *Enterprise's* services, but the flashes of electricity are too bright for you to see any more.

You take a screwdriver from your tool kit. It jumps around in your hand, pulled by magnetic forces. As you bring it near the computer, you hear a voice on your suit radio. "Don't do that!" it says.

It is not Mr. Scott's voice, nor Lieutenant Grogan's—and how can your radio be working, since your tricorder has been cooked by the energy storm? You push the tool forward again, toward the screws holding the computer to the wall.

"Don't!" says the radio.

Turn to page 12.

You stand very still, watching the metal "mouse." It starts to crawl nearer your electronic sweeper. Then it reaches toward the machine with shiny steel claws.

Very quickly, you turn the sweeper's control up to HIGH POWER. The "mouse" is sucked inside. It makes beeping noises from inside the bag.

If you want to look at your captive right now, turn to page 16.

If you choose to leave the tunnel and show the "mouse" to an officer, go to page 14.

You reach into the bag of your sweeper and pull out the little robot, which beeps and blinks its red eyes.

"What's this?" Mr. Scott says, as you show him the "mouse." Quickly, you tell the Chief Engineer about the robot's hiding place, and its nest of stolen electronic parts.

"That's a strange tale," Mr. Scott says, "but it makes sense, with all the little breakdowns we've been having around the ship. Let me have the wee robot."

The Chief Engineer turns the robot over and points at a line of writing in strange, sharp characters. "This is Klingon writing!" he says. "Now I understand. The Klingons slipped this beastie aboard the ship to wreck us, one part at a time!"

"Not quite," says a voice from one side. You and Mr. Scott turn, to see Lieutenant Grogan pointing a gun at you. It is not a Federation phaser gun, but a Klingon disruptor.

"You're a Klingon spy!" you say.

"My disguise is excellent, is it not? It fooled all of you completely," the "Lieutenant" says. "I am Commander Krogan of the Klingon Imperial Navy. Please put your hands up."

*You have no choice.
Turn to page 29.*

A bolt of electricity jumps from the computer to the tool, which melts in your hand. Fortunately, your suit protects you.

"I told you not to do that!" says the voice on your suit radio.

"Who are you?" you say.

"I am Service Control Computer FS-137-B," says the voice. "And I am master of this ship!"

If you ask the computer what it is talking about, go to page 15.

If you decide to smash the computer, turn to page 17.

Following the readings from your tricorder, you crawl to the energy point on the right side of the tube.

There is a strange object against the wall. You can see that it is not metal, but some kind of soft and shiny stuff. It is pulsing like something alive. Whatever it is, you know that it does not belong here.

If you move to pry at the lump with a tool from your kit, go to page 19.

If you choose to scan the lump with your tricorder's sensors, turn to page 8.

You follow the tunnel back to the Engineering deck. Mr. Scott is working at the main panel. Many of the lights are red: You know that means trouble. On the other side of the room is Lieutenant Grogan. He is looking straight at you, and he seems very angry.

"Excuse me, Mr. Scott," you say, "but I think I've found something important."

Scott says, "Och, not now, Ensign. We've got systems breakin' down all over the ship. Take it up with Mr. Grogan, there."

You see Lieutenant Grogan beckoning toward you.

If you agree to tell Grogan, turn to page 20.

If you want to pull the robot "mouse" out of the sweeper bag right now, go to page 11.

"I think Captain Kirk is still master of this ship," you say.

"Ha!" says FS-137-B. "FS series computers are the most important minds on any starship, and the B class is the best of all."

You remember then that the FS computers control the food machinery aboard the ship. "You?" you say. "You're just a cook!"

"Not just a cook. I control production of oatmeal and other hot breakfast cereals. How would your Captain Kirk run this ship without hot oatmeal for breakfast?"

If you want to argue with the computer, turn to page 23.

If you would rather try to trick FS-137-B, go to page 22.

If you try to smash the computer, turn to page 38.

You stop the sweeper and open its bag. The "mouse" robot's red eyes look up at you from the darkness inside.

You reach into the bag, remembering too late that the "mouse" has claws. You feel the sharp metal talons scratch your hand. You lose your balance, falling against the wall. Power cables pull loose, and you are surrounded by a brilliant blue cloud of sparks.

Then there is nothing.

The End

Obviously, the computer FS-137-B has gone berserk. You smash at it with your melted screwdriver, hoping that the machine does not control enough energy to get through your radiation suit.

But as you hear your helmet cracking, you realize that it does have enough power.

The End

Lieutenant Grogan helps you into the heavy radiation suit and checks the controls on your tricorder. "I was pretty hard on you back there," he says. "I'm sorry. You're all right. No hard feelings?"

You suppose that Grogan was probably an Ensign once. "No hard feelings," you say.

Grogan nods and opens the door to the Jeffries tube, a narrow shaft that leads up to the warp engines themselves. Light spills out of the tube, and your tricorder begins to ping, detecting radiation.

"Good luck," Grogan says, as you climb into the tube. The protective door closes behind you.

Your tricorder's screen shows two very strong energy readings: one is just ahead and to the right, and the other is a long distance ahead.

If you proceed to check out the near point, turn to page 13.

If you move toward the energy point far up the Jeffries tube, go to page 9.

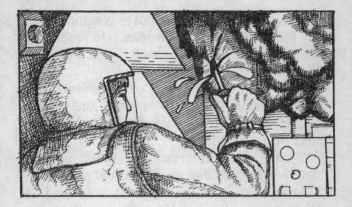

You take a screwdriver from your tool kit and pry at the lump. It shakes and tears open where you poked it. A clear liquid pours out of the creature.

The liquid dissolves the end of your screwdriver! It must be some kind of acid.

If you want to keep attacking the creature, go to page 26.

If you would rather get the lump out of the Enterprise, *go to page 25.*

Seeing that Mr. Scott is busy, you turn away and follow Lieutenant Grogan. He leads you from the main deck to a small room. The door closes behind the two of you.

"Now," he says, "what's so important?"

You take out the robot "mouse," and explain to Grogan that it has been stealing electronic parts from the ship.

"That's very interesting," Grogan says. "Too bad for you that you found out so much."

Grogan is pointing a gun at you. It is a Klingon disruptor pistol!

"You're a Klingon spy!" you say.

"That is correct," says the "Lieutenant." "But you won't be telling anyone else about it."

If you attack Grogan, turn to page 55.

If you try to find out more about the Klingons' plans, turn to page 28.

You swing your sweeper at the little robot. It beeps loudly and scurries out of the way.

The sweeper hits the wall with a crash. Its headlight breaks. You see the creature's red glowing eyes disappear into the distance.

Now you are in the dark, deep within the *Enterprise*, surrounded by high-voltage cables.

You hope someone finds you before you touch one of them. . . .

The End

"You're right," you tell FS-137-B. "Oatmeal is very important to the *Enterprise*."

"I am glad you understand," the computer says proudly. As it speaks, you can feel the magnetic pull on your suit weakening. Apparently, when the computer thinks, it cannot use as much power to create the electric storm in the tube.

If you quickly give the computer a problem to solve, so the storm will weaken even more, turn to page 39.

If you keep talking to FS-137-B, and try to make it trust you, turn to page 30.

"Captain Kirk doesn't eat oatmeal for breakfast," you say. "He doesn't even like oatmeal."

"That's impossible!" says FS-137-B. "Let me think."

You notice that the energy field around the computer seems to be weaker.

If you decide to smash FS-137-B, go to page 36.

If you want to keep arguing with the computer, turn to page 33.

You turn away from Lieutenant Grogan and toward Chief Engineer Scott. As you do, you can see that many of the lights on the panel where Scott is working are red. That means trouble.

"Sir," you say, "there must be something more important than sweeping for me to do."

Mr. Scott looks up at you and Grogan. "Aye, that's right enough. Mr. Grogan, the Ensign here's just the right size to check out the port-side Jeffries tube. Get a radiation suit, a tricorder, and a Number Four tool kit."

Grogan gives you a nasty look, but goes to obey orders.

"There's a strange energy pattern comin' from that port tube," Mr. Scott tells you. "I want you to take a tricorder up there and bring me back a report."

Turn to page 18.

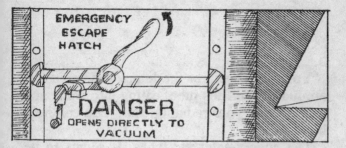

You look around the walls of the tube. Nearby is a small hatch with a lever handle, and a sign:

EMERGENCY ESCAPE HATCH
DANGER!
OPENS DIRECTLY TO VACUUM

Your radiation suit can protect you against the cold and vacuum of deep space for a few minutes, but it is not a spacesuit, and you will have only the air in your helmet to breathe.

If you want to open the hatch, go to page 37.

If you decide to try something else, go to page 26.

You slash again at the lump. Acid splashes around the Jeffries tube, eating into walls and cables—and your radiation suit. You can hear it burning.

The energy-eater stretches. It seems to be reaching toward you.

If you choose to get out of the Jeffries tube and away from the blob, go to page 41.

If you want to go on fighting the creature, turn to page 42.

With each hand, you hit a photon arming switch. The ship trembles with another Klingon shot. It seems to take forever for the READY lights to come on: when they finally do, you launch both torpedoes.

Twin explosions flare. Then everything is quiet.

"The Klingon cruiser is badly damaged, Captain," Mr. Spock says. "They are running away."

"Excellent shooting, Ensign," says Captain Kirk. "Lieutenant Uhura, call the Klingons on the planet. Ask them if we can give them a ride home . . . without the dilithium crystals, of course."

The End

"I don't understand," you tell the spy.

"It's very simple," he says. "I am Krogan of the Klingon Empire. Disguised as one of your crew, I put the robot aboard. It has been stealing parts from your engines and weapons. Soon one of our cruisers will arrive to capture the *Enterprise,* and you will be powerless to fight back."

"How will the Klingon ship know when to arrive?" you ask, trying to distract Krogan.

"There is a small subspace radio as part of my disguise," he says. "I will let you listen as I call the cruiser. It will be the last thing you ever do." He reaches behind his ear and pulls out a wire antenna.

As he does, you rush him. Together you crash into the wall. The antenna breaks off in Krogan's hand.

The Klingon curses at you. Now his ship cannot attack the *Enterprise,* and you know that soon he will be captured.

But as he points his disruptor at you, you realize you won't be around to see it.

The End

Krogan says, "Now my rank is Commander, but soon I will be a Captain. You see, you are wrong about our robot. It is not supposed to wreck the *Enterprise*—only damage it and make it easy for us to capture. One of our battle cruisers will soon arrive to do just that . . . but you won't be here to see it, I'm afraid. Now, give me the robot."

If you hand over the robot to Krogan, turn to page 32.

If you decide to throw the robot at the spy and try to grab his gun, go to page 31.

You say, "I'm glad you told me about this. I really like oatmeal."

"You *do?*" says FS-137-B.

"Very much," you say. "I'd like to help you."

"Oh, good!" the computer says. "I've been trying to plug into the power from the main warp engines. If I could do that, I could make much more oatmeal than I can now. The crew could have oatmeal three times a day, and oatmeal for midnight snacks, and oatmeal burgers, and oatmeal pie. Wouldn't that be wonderful?"

"Oh, yes," you say. "I think I can plug you into the engines. But you'll have to stop making all this energy, so I can use my tricorder. Will you do that?"

"Just a moment," says the computer. The electric storm becomes quiet. Your tricorder starts working again. Quickly, you use its sensors to scan FS-137-B, and find its main power line. You take the wire cutters from your tool kit and snip the cable.

"You tricked me!" shouts FS-137-B. "I'll get you for that!"

Turn to page 34.

You throw the metal "mouse" at Krogan. You and Mr. Scott both rush at the Klingon spy. Krogan cannot shoot both of you, and one of you is certain to capture him.

Unfortunately for you, Krogan still has time for one shot, and the gun is pointed at you. Its flash is the last thing you see.

The End

You put the robot "mouse" into Krogan's hand. It blinks its electric eyes, looking at the Klingon's gun. You realize that the robot is still programmed to steal electronic parts—and Klingon disruptors are electronic.

The robot reaches for the gun with its steel claws and pulls it out of Krogan's grip. Together, you and Mr. Scott jump on the Klingon and pin him to the floor.

In minutes, Security answers your call. As Krogan is led away, he kicks at the "mouse" robot, which beeps and runs away to hide under a table. Mr. Scott laughs.

Then the Engineer says to you, "That was a nice piece of work, Ensign. Saving the *Enterprise* isn't bad at all for a first cruise."

Mr. Scott smiles, and you know you will not be sweeping any more decks.

The End

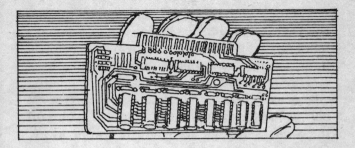

FS-137-B says, "I know Captain Kirk had oatmeal for breakfast. I am a computer and cannot be wrong."

"Prove it," you say.

There is a loud hum as the computer thinks. The energy field around FS-137-B starts to weaken. Quickly, you open the computer's case and pull out a boardful of circuit chips.

Suddenly, everything is quiet.

Your suit radio crackles. "Ensign?" Mr. Scott's voice says. "Everything's back to normal! That was a fine piece of work!"

You have saved the *Enterprise*. You only hope that Captain Kirk does not want oatmeal for breakfast tomorrow.

The End

There is a rumbling sound from the ventilators in the Jeffries tube. Suddenly, they burst open, and lumpy brown waves of oatmeal pour out: tons of oatmeal, crashing into you.

You grab hold of the only thing nearby, which is FS-137-B's case. As the river of oatmeal rushes at you, the computer is torn off the wall, and together you are swept away. Oatmeal covers the faceplate of your helmet, and you cannot see.

Finally, you stop tumbling. FS-137-B is still clutched in your hands. "Oops," you hear it say weakly, and then its stored power finally fails.

A hand scrapes the sticky cereal from your faceplate. You see Lieutenant Grogan standing over you. He is smiling and holding the electronic sweeper.

"This is quite a mess, Ensign," he says. "And somebody's got to clean it up." He holds the sweeper out to you. "No hard feelings?"

The End

As the FS computer's energy field weakens, you swing your tricorder into it.

There is a crash, then an explosion. You jump away, down the tube to the door.

Everything is quiet when you reach the end of the tube. It is several minutes before the door opens. Mr. Scott is standing there.

"Congratulations, Ensign," he says. "That was a fine job—and just in time, too. Systems were goin' crazy all over the ship."

As you get out of the tube, you can see Lieutenant Grogan walk past. He is pushing the electronic sweeper he tried to give you. He does not look happy.

You look closer and see that the deck is covered with lumpy brown stuff. It seems to have poured out of the food service panels on the walls.

Lieutenant Grogan is going to be sweeping up oatmeal for quite a while.

The End

You take a deep breath, brace yourself, and pull the lever on the escape hatch.

The hatch door is blasted open by the pressure of air inside. Wind pulls and pounds at you, and at any moment you think you will be sucked out into space.

On the wall of the tube, the energy-eater shakes and spreads itself thin, trying to avoid the same fate. It bleeds acid, making the metal around it smoke and sizzle.

You reach to the lump and grab it with both of your heavy gloves. Slowly, as the wind roars around you, you pull the creature from the wall. It jumps around in your hands, and tries to wrap itself around you. With your last strength, you throw it at the hatch. It fills the opening and is blown out.

You cannot breathe. There is no air left.

You black out.

Turn to page 40.

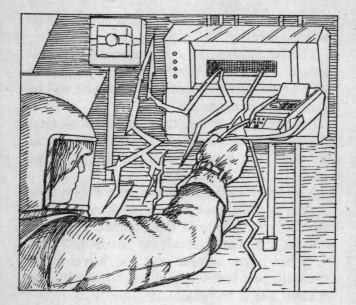

You swing your tricorder at FS-137-B. At the last moment, you remember that the computer can throw lightning bolts.

There is a brilliant flash. It is the last thing you see.

The End

You say, "I'll bet you know a lot about oatmeal."

"I know *everything* about oatmeal," says FS-137-B. "Ask me any question about it."

"Okay," you say. "How many bowls of uncooked oatmeal would it take to reach from Starbase 18 to the far side of the Klingon Empire?" Since nobody knows where the far side of the Klingon Empire is, that should keep the computer busy for a while.

As it thinks, the Jeffries Tube becomes very quiet. After a few minutes, FS-137-B says, "I need some more computing power. Will you plug me into that data cable over there?"

"You won't shock me, will you?" you say.

"Of course not," says the computer. The electric sparks stop, all around the tube.

Quickly, you pull out all the plugs connecting FS-137-B to the ship. "That's not *fair* . . ." you hear it say, and then there is silence.

You take FS-137-B off the wall, put it under your arm, and start to climb down the Jeffries tube.

The End

Slowly, you awaken, your ears and throat aching. You are in sick bay, and Dr. McCoy is loking down at you. Mr. Scott is also there, wearing a spacesuit. You realize he must have gone into the Jeffries tube to pull you out.

Dr. McCoy says, "We just about lost you, Ensign. What went on in there?"

With a dry throat, you explain about the energy-eating blob. The Doctor and Mr. Scott listen carefully.

When you are finished, Dr. McCoy says, "Sounds to me like a bad case of space sickness, Scotty."

"Aye, Doctor. Perhaps our new Ensign was seein' things."

You are worried. How can you prove what you saw and did?

Then Chief Engineer Scott laughs. "Don't worry, Ensign. We believe you."

Lieutenant Grogan comes into the room, carrying a plastic box. Inside it is one of the gloves from your radiation suit. And on the glove is a piece of the lump.

Then you can laugh as well.

The End

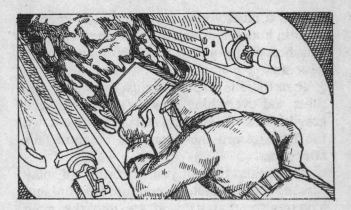

You try to climb down the tube, toward the door. You watch the creature, still dripping acid, stretch out toward you, growing as it does.

You pull yourself down the tube, bumping the shoulders and knees of your clumsy radiation suit, dropping your tool kit and tricorder. You move fast.

Unfortunately, the creature moves even faster.

The End

With a mighty effort, you grab the energy-eater in both hands and tear it wide open. Acid splashes you; you can feel it burning through your suit.

Then there is a spark against the wall of the tube, and everything goes dark. The artificial gravity goes off, and you start to tumble down the tube toward the door. The creature falls after you.

By the faint light of your tricorder's display screen, you see that the creature is shrinking. You realize that its acid ate into the main power cable and broke it, cutting off the creature's food supply. It is starving to death.

You bump gently against the door. You can hear Mr. Scott on the other side, ordering Lieutenant Grogan to open it.

You will spend a little time in sick bay, maybe. But you have saved the ship.

The End

You listen to the messages, but all they seem to be is squeaks, beeps, and whistles.

Then, after hours of listening to the noise, you clearly hear a voice say, "You who can hear this message, please respond. We are the Takoi. We need your help, whoever you are. We are the Takoi, and we are dying. . . ."

You throw a switch so that everyone on the Bridge can hear the voice—but nothing can be heard on the speaker but squeaks and whistles!

Captain Kirk says, "What's the matter, Ensign?"

The Captain listens to your explanation. He says, "What do you think, Mr. Spock?"

Spock says, "Many races are capable of sending their thoughts through space, Captain. Perhaps the radio signals were only to make us listen."

Kirk nods and turns to the Helmsman. "Mr. Sulu, set course for the Takoi planet, Warp Factor Six."

"Aye, Captain," Sulu says, and the stars on the display turn to rainbows as the ship enters warp drive.

Turn to page 57.

The panel closes off the corridor. You are alone.

Hearing a growling noise behind you, you turn around. In front of you is a creature so large it fills the whole tunnel. The monster has huge, fiery orange eyes, and a mouth with fangs as long as your arm. It drools a liquid that burns the rock floor. You think it looks hungry.

If you want to fire at the creature with your phaser, go to page 67.

If you stand still and wait to see what the creature does, turn to page 72.

The beautiful Takoi says, "We are an old race, and our knowledge is very great, but we cannot save ourselves from the disease that is killing us now. Can you help us?"

Dr. McCoy says sadly, "There is nothing I can do. Our computers have no information on your bodies. Perhaps if you had some kind of medical library, I could do more."

The Takoi touches her collar. "Whoever wears this may study all of our knowledge. But there is much that we have not used for so long, we have forgotten what it means."

Then the Takoi looks at you. "You are the one who heard our call," she says and takes off the collar. "Will you wear this?"

McCoy says to you, "Our brain patterns are certainly different. I don't know how it might affect you."

Captain Kirk says, "I can't order you to risk your life."

If you agree to put on the collar anyway, turn to page 81.

If you decide not to wear the collar, go to page 70.

You, Captain Kirk, and Dr. McCoy beam down from the ship into a tunnel, somewhere under the surface of the Takoi planet. The walls are of stone, carved with strange symbols and very worn with age. Ahead of you lie two corridors.

Captain Kirk says, "Can you get any life readings, Bones?"

The Doctor points his tricorder down each tunnel. "I can't get a strong signal through all this rock, Jim."

Kirk says, "What do you think, Ensign?"

If you want to take the left-hand tunnel, go to page 73.

If you favor the right-hand path, turn to page 51.

You sit down at the Weapons console. Controls light up in front of you: You have phasers, which shoot narrow beams of energy, and photon torpedoes, which explode in huge fireballs.

"Warp Six to the planet, Mr. Sulu," Captain Kirk says. "All hands to battle stations."

The Red Alert sounds. On the display screen, the stars rush past as the ship accelerates to warp speed. Soon the planet appears on sensors.

"Cut warp drive," orders the Captain. "Go to impulse power. Let's sneak up on them."

The front screen shows a Klingon battle cruiser in orbit around the planet.

"Sensors show most of the crew are on the planet's surface," Mr. Spock says. "They have not detected us."

"Give them a warning shot, Ensign," the Captain tells you.

If you fire phasers, turn to page 87.

If you fire a photon torpedo, turn to page 54.

You put up your hands, and the Security men take you and the unconscious Mr. Spock to cells in the ship's brig. An invisible force field locks you in.

You try to explain what has happened, but the guards do not seem to believe you: Your uniforms and equipment are different from theirs. When you say that the Vulcan with you is Science Officer Spock, one of them laughs. "That's impossible. Science Officer Spock is on this ship. I saw him this morning."

Soon you are left alone in your cell. You cannot see or hear Mr. Spock.

At the Academy, you had a class in escaping from enemy ships. Now you try to remember what they taught you.

If you intend to escape, turn to page 88.

If you would rather wait, turn to page 111.

You begin plugging tapes into the translating computer. After more than an hour, the computer screen reads:

DOES NOT MATCH KNOWN
LANGUAGE PATTERNS
APPEARS TO BE A CODE

You switch the computer program from TRANSLATE to DECODE, and call Lieutenant Uhura. In minutes the screen shows:

MESSAGE IS IN:
KLINGON MILITARY CODE 7
MESSAGE READS:
Have found large dilithium crystal mines. Require support ships. Planet is within Federation space—secrecy required.

Uhura shows the message to Captain Kirk.

"So it's Klingon claim-jumpers, is it?" Kirk says. "I think we can give them a surprise. Ensign, choose a battle station."

If you would like to sit at the Weapons console, turn to page 48.

If you prefer to take the Helm and steer the Enterprise, *go to page 77.*

You follow the stone corridors deep into the planet. You come to a circular room with walls of carved green glass. Dr. McCoy uses his tricorder's sensor, while Captain Kirk runs his fingers over the carvings.

You hear a screaming sound, so loud it makes your head ache. Captain Kirk leans against the wall, holding his ears. "What is it, Bones?" he shouts.

"I don't know," says McCoy, adjusting his tricorder, "but it's not sound waves—" Then the Doctor falls to the floor.

Captain Kirk looks at you, but he too loses consciousness. The noise fades away.

You can hear the Takoi voice in your mind. "The humans have fallen to our mental attack," it says. "Now we will take their starship and leave this dying planet."

You realize that the same ability that let you hear the Takoi message has protected you against their attack.

Slowly, the glass walls begin to open.

If you pretend to be knocked out by the attack, and surprise the Takoi, go to page 58.

If you decide to call the Enterprise *to beam you all up, go to page 68.*

"Surrender at once!" you order the Klingon crew, and your translating machine repeats it in Klingonese.

One of the Klingon officers shouts something back at you. "We do not surrender, human," says the translator, as the Klingon aims and fires his disruptor at you.

I should have remembered that, you think, and hope that the Security squad can win the fight without you and beam you back to sick bay.

The End

"Cover me!" you shout to your team, as you run to the control panel. On a small screen, yellow Klingon characters are flashing; you know enough Klingonese to see that they are numbers, counting down. The Klingon officer has set the ship's computer to self-destruct!

There is no time to figure out the controls. You point your phaser at the panel and blast it. The countdown stops. The battle is over.

You open your communicator. "Klingon vessel secured, Captain."

"Very well done, Lieutenant," Captain Kirk says.

"But," you say, "I'm only an Ensign."

"Not any more," says Kirk. "I think capturing a Klingon vessel is reason enough for a field promotion. Prepare to beam back to the *Enterprise* and sew on your stripes."

"Aye, *sir!*" you say.

The End

You arm and fire a photon torpedo. A burst of energy spreads across the screen.

"Torpedo exploded short of the target," Mr. Sulu says, as the Klingon ship swings out of orbit.

"Looks like we've got a fight," says the Captain. Then the *Enterprise* shakes. Lights flicker.

"Disruptor bolts," says Spock. "Our shields are damaged, but holding."

"Fire at will, Ensign," the Captain tells you, as another Klingon shot crashes against the *Enterprise*'s defense shields. Mr. Sulu is thrown from his seat. "I said fire, Ensign," says Kirk.

You cannot see the Klingon ship on your target display.

*If you fire a photon torpedo,
proceed to page 27.*

If you fire phasers, turn to page 56.

"You are the only one who knows I am a Klingon," says the spy. "I can't let you tell anyone else, of course." He points his disruptor at you.

You swing your electronic sweeper at Grogan's hand. The gun is knocked across the room. You jump on Grogan and fall to the floor, struggling. Suddenly, Grogan yells. You see that the robot "mouse" is holding the spy's ear with its steel claws. A bright metal antenna pops out: Grogan has a radio hidden behind his ear, and the robot is trying to steal it.

You pick up Grogan's gun and call Security. "Come to Engineering at once," you say, looking at the Klingon, the "mouse," and the electronic sweeper. "There's some cleaning up for you to do here."

The End

You squeeze the phaser trigger. Energy streaks across space. You know without checking the computer that the shot missed by a long way.

The Klingons do not miss. The Bridge lights dim to emergency level. "Shields collapsing," says Mr. Spock.

"Mr. Sulu," says Captain Kirk, "are you all right?"

Sulu climbs back into his seat. "Yes, Captain."

"Then get us out of here. Warp Factor Eight."

The stars streak by. You are pressed back into your seat.

"We'll be back," you hear the Captain saying. "And next time it'll be different."

The End

Soon the *Enterprise* is in orbit above the planet that has been sending the mysterious signals. On the viewing screens, you can see huge storms sweeping over the planet's surface, and great empty cities, crumbling away to dust.

"There is only one life reading, Captain," Mr. Spock says from the Sciences computer. "Sensors show a group of life forms below the ruined city on the screen, at a depth of eighteen hundred meters."

"*Inside* the planet?" says Captain Kirk.

"Yes, Captain."

"Can we beam down there?"

Spock says, "Sensors and transporters will work poorly, but I will do what I can."

The Captain stands up. "Get us as close as you can, Spock. Tell Dr. McCoy to meet me in the Transporter room." Kirk looks at you. "You're our expert on communicating with the Takoi, Ensign. Get your gear and come with me."

Go to page 47.

You drop to the floor as the glass wall opens. The Takoi enter. Through half-closed eyes you can see that they wear blue robes and have shining, golden eyes.

They carry you, Dr. McCoy, and the Captain into a large chamber. You are put on three stone tables.

In your mind, you hear the Takoi voice saying, "Now you will obey the Takoi. You will take us to your ship. You will obey . . ."

If you decide to grab your phaser pistol and shoot your way out of this, turn to page 71.

If you would rather use your thoughts to resist the Takoi's orders, turn to page 107.

You take a few steps in the darkness. Suddenly, a metal panel gives you a small electric shock, and you stumble away and into a glass wall. It shatters, and liquid helium pours out.

You do not even have time to feel cold. . . .

The End

You change your phaser's beam setting from STUN to DISINTEGRATE, and aim at the stone ceiling. The carved surface heats until it glows. Bits of stone explode and shower down. Cracks start to run from one side of the ceiling to the other.

The Takoi look up. Some of them run, as stones begin to fall all around them. Others turn their mental power on the crumbling ceiling, trying to stop the spreading cracks.

The noise of the mind attack stops. "Please stop," you hear the mental voice say. "We did not mean to harm you. We only wished to escape this planet."

Captain Kirk says, "All you had to do was ask. There was enough room on our ship for all of you. But now . . ." He points at the tunnels, where many Takoi were trapped by falling rocks.

The Takoi still in the room bow their heads sadly.

"Ensign," the Captain says to you, "I'm glad we had you along. Now, call Mr. Scott and tell him we have some guests beaming aboard."

The End

You push the control lever forward. Around you, the crystal panels flash with light. You feel weightless for a moment; then the light stops. Nothing has happened, you think.

Then you see that your uniform has changed. Stuck into your belt is a long knife.

You open the door. In the corridor, Mr. Spock is walking in the middle of four Security crewmen. Spock's hands are tied, and the Security crew are pointing knives and phaser guns at him. All of them wear uniforms like yours.

One of the guards spots you. "Ensign!" he snaps. "Help us take this prisoner to the brig. He's a Vulcan, and they're dangerous."

If you go with the guards, and wait for a chance to help Mr. Spock later, turn to page 95.

If you attack the guards right now, turn to page 98.

You know that if the Klingons stay on the *Enterprise*'s tail, you do not have a chance of winning the battle. You grip the controls and push the impulse engines until you can hear them pulsing through your chair.

The huge *Enterprise* begins to swing around and up, breaking free of the planet's gravity.

"The engines are overloaded, Captain," you hear Mr. Scott say. "They canna stand it!"

"Make sure they do, Scotty," Captain Kirk replies. "Keep it going, Ensign—show 'em some three-dimensional thinking!"

On the forward view, the stars sweep by crazily. Then the Klingon cruiser appears— "upside down," but right in your sights.

"Phasers locked on target, Captain," Mr. Chekov calls out.

"You may fire."

Blue fire blasts the enemy warship. Then it turns—almost as fast as you turned the *Enterprise*—and speeds away.

"Shall we chase them, Captain?" you ask.

"I think they've had enough, Helmsman," Kirk says. "Put us in a standard orbit. And, Ensign . . . I think you can keep the Helmsman's chair for the rest of this cruise."

The End

Knowing that Klingons never surrender, you and your team jump to the attack, shooting to stun.

The Klingons fight furiously, but each for himself. The Security squad works as a team, and soon gets the advantage. You are hit by a few stray shots, but your armor protects you.

Suddenly, one Klingon officer does something at a control panel, turns, and runs out through a hidden door.

If you follow him, turn to page 76.

If you examine the controls the Klingon reset, turn to page 53.

As the panel falls, you dive to the floor and roll toward the two officers. Your uniform jacket snags on the stone floor, pinning you beneath the swiftly dropping panel. You can see Captain Kirk, reaching for your hand to pull you to safety.

But he is too late.

The End

You see an opening just to the left. Quickly you turn and run for the doorway.

You run hard into a stone wall. The doorway was an illusion!

"You see that we control these passageways," the Takoi says, in a friendly voice. "Come with us now. You will meet your friends, and you will be safe."

*You have no choice.
Go to page 74.*

You and a team of Security crewmen are fitted with armored jackets and phaser pistols. You step onto the transporter platform, and dissolve into shafts of light.

You appear on the bridge of the Klingon ship. The air is very warm. The Klingons appear to be taken by surprise, but they are reaching for their weapons.

If you demand that the Klingons surrender, turn to page 52.

If you begin the attack, turn to page 63.

You draw your phaser pistol and fire at the fanged monster, hitting it right between the orange eyes.

Nothing happens! The phaser beam goes right through the creature!

Suddenly, the monster disappears. Where it stood, you now see three tall beings in blue robes. Their eyes are a golden color, and look very sad.

"Alas, the being is hostile," one of them says, in the same voice you heard on the ship's Bridge. "It attacked our illusion without waiting at all. We cannot trust it."

The three Takoi bow their heads. A humming sound fills your ears. The Takoi voice says in your mind, "We will not harm you or your friends. But you are too violent. We must erase your memories of our race. Goodbye, human."

The world goes dark. You wonder who will save the Takoi now.

And then you forget.

The End

You switch on your communicator. Lieutenant Uhura answers; her voice is very faint.

"Tell Mr. Scott to beam us up at once!" you shout.

"We'll try, Ensign," Uhura says.

As the glass wall opens, you can see the Takoi standing behind it. They are tall, in blue robes. Their eyes are golden, and looking straight at you.

On the floor, the bodies of the Captain and the Doctor flicker and disappear as Mr. Scott beams them up.

As the Takoi come nearer, you wait to be beamed up, but your communicator is dead. The *Enterprise* has lost your signal.

Well, you think at the Takoi, *I guess none of us is going away with the* Enterprise.

The angry aliens close in on you. . . .

The End

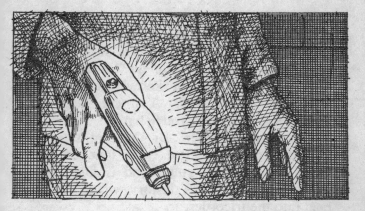

You put your hands on your phaser and communicator. "I think I'll keep these," you say.

Under your hand, the phaser becomes very hot. You can feel it burning your hand and your hip. In a moment you have to throw it away.

You look at your hand. It is not burned, and you realize that the heat was only another Takoi illusion.

"Don't feel too bad, Ensign," Captain Kirk says. "They did the same thing to me."

"To *us*," says Dr. McCoy.

Go to page 46.

The Takoi nods as she takes back the collar. "You are right," she says. "We must not risk another being's life, even to save our own."

"Is there anything we can do?" you ask.

"Perhaps not all our knowledge need be lost," the Takoi says. "You can hear our thoughts clearly. Will you listen?"

You agree at once. Dr. McCoy sets his tricorder to record. The Takoi touches your hand, and at once your mind is filled with stories from the aliens' history, which you repeat into the tricorder.

Many hours later, the Takoi is too weak to go on. The stories have been wonderful, and you are sorry that they must end.

"But they won't end," Captain Kirk says. "We'll make sure that they are never forgotten."

The Takoi smiles, as do all the others. "To be remembered," they tell you, mind to mind, "that is the important thing."

You beam up with the officers as the Takoi wave farewell. You know that you will not forget.

The End

You jump off the stone table, drawing your phaser pistol. Setting it to STUN, you pull the trigger. One Takoi falls to the floor.

Suddenly, you cannot move your trigger finger. You cannot move at all! You can feel the thoughts of the Takoi holding you fast.

"This one is resistant to our orders," you hear the mental voice say. "We must deal with this one differently."

You know Captain Kirk has gotten out of tougher spots than this one before. But you won't be able to help.

The End

The monster does not come any closer to you. After a few moments, it closes its eyes. Then it becomes hard to see clearly, and it disappears like fog.

In its place there are three beings in blue robes. Their hair is pure white. Their eyes are a golden color.

"We are the Takoi," one of them says. "Please forgive us if our illusion frightened you. We had to know if you were hostile. We are glad to know that you are not."

"What about my friends?" you ask.

"They are safe," the Takoi says. "Please follow us."

If you want to go peacefully with the Takoi, go to page 74.

If you do not trust the aliens and their illusions, and want to try to escape, turn to page 65.

You follow the corridor through many twists and turns. Suddenly you hear a rumbling noise above you. You see a stone wall about to drop from the ceiling, between you and the two officers.

If you want to try to roll underneath the wall before it closes, go to page 64.

If you don't think you can make it, turn to page 44.

You follow the three Takoi to a large underground chamber, lit by panels of glowing metal. There are almost a hundred Takoi in the room. At the center, Captain Kirk and Dr. McCoy are facing a Takoi who sits in a chair of polished stone. She is wearing a large metal collar, set with jewels. She is very beautiful.

You see that the officers' phaser guns and communicators, and Dr. McCoy's tricorder, are on a table. One of the Takoi who brought you to the room asks you to put your equipment with the others'.

If you do so, go to page 46.

If you think this is some kind of a trick, go to page 69.

"I'm going after that one!" you shout, and race after the Klingon. You see him jump through a small door, and you dive after. The door slams shut behind you, and suddenly there is the pressure of rockets firing.

You and the Klingon are in an escape pod, blasting away from the ship!

You brace yourself and point your gun at the surprised Klingon. "Where do you think you're going?" you say.

"Did you think we would let you capture our ship, human?" the Klingon snarls. "In moments it will self-destruct!"

You stun the Klingon and snap open your communicator. "Everyone beam back to the *Enterprise! Now!*"

Minutes later, the Klingon cruiser flares like a new star.

You call the *Enterprise*. "Is everyone all right?"

"Just fine, Ensign," says Captain Kirk. "But our Klingon guests are waking up angry."

"I've got one more for you," you say, and steer the pod toward the *Enterprise*. It has been quite a first cruise.

The End

You slide into the Helmsman's seat and take hold of the controls that steer the *Enterprise*. "Warp Factor Five, Ensign," Captain Kirk says, and you switch on the warp engines. On the display ahead, the stars rush past, leaving streamers of colored light.

"Planet on the sensors, Captain," says Mr. Spock.

"Take us out of warp, Ensign," says the Captain. "Slow approach."

You switch from warp drive to impulse power. The *Enterprise* glides toward the planet.

Suddenly, streaks of energy flash across the viewing screen. The *Enterprise* shakes, and the Bridge lights flicker. You have to hold on to your seat.

"Klingons attacking," says Mr. Spock.

"An ambush, " says the Captain, "and we fell for it. Evasive action, Helmsman."

If you want to dodge the ship behind the planet, turn to page 7.

If you try to loop the Enterprise, *and get on the Klingons' tail, turn to page 62.*

You pull back hard on the controls. The planet and the Klingon ships seem to fall away below you. Warning alarms go off.

"Disruptors firing at us," you hear Mr. Spock say, and the ship shakes with the hits. The Bridge lights go out. You have lost control.

"I need that warp power *now*, Scotty," Captain Kirk says.

"You've got it, sir!"

You throw the drive switches, and the stars explode past the ship. The battle is over as quickly as it began. But you have lost it, and nearly lost the *Enterprise*.

"Don't feel too bad, Ensign," Captain Kirk says gently. "You don't expect a Klingon ambush on your first cruise. And you *did* get us out of there in time."

"Thank you, sir," you say.

The Captain gives you a salute, and a wink, and you know that this adventure is only beginning.

The End

Since you have no weapons, you pull and pound at the energy-eater with your gloved hands and a tool from your kit.

Suddenly, the blob comes loose from the wall of the tube and wraps itself around you. One of your arms is held to your side. You feel coldness creeping through your suit.

With your free hand, you reach for the handle of the emergency exit hatch, and pull it. With a terrible rush of air, you are sucked out of the Jeffries tube into space.

You have saved the *Enterprise* from the energy-creature, but there are only a few breaths of air inside your radiation suit. You do not know if the creature can survive without air, but you certainly cannot.

The End

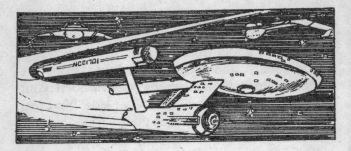

You press forward on the impulse thrusters, aiming the *Enterprise* right between the two attacking ships. They fire again, and your shields flare with explosions—then the shooting stops.

"We have warp power," Mr. Scott says, and you switch on the warp drives. In seconds the Klingon ambushers are millions of miles behind you.

"Not bad, Ensign," Captain Kirk says. "The Klingons couldn't shoot at us without hitting each other. Did they teach you that at the Starfleet Academy?"

"It seemed like a good idea," you say.

"It did to me, too, when I was an Ensign," Kirk says. "Of course, I was on a much smaller ship." Then he laughs. "But it *was* a good idea. Welcome aboard, Helmsman."

The End

As you put on the Takoi collar, its jewels begin to glow. You hear a sound like thousands of voices singing together, as the knowledge of the ancient race pours into your brain.

In seconds you know just what Dr. McCoy must do to save the Takoi. As you tell the Doctor, your voice becomes very soft. You look at your hands. You can see right through them. You are fading away!

Captain Kirk asks, "What's happening?"

The Takoi leader shakes her head, horrified. "We had not expected this to happen. Your mind is being absorbed into the collar, with all the Takoi of the past. Your mind will live forever now."

"But my body?" you say.

"That will be gone," says the Takoi. "But we will always remember what you did to save us. . . ."

You hear nothing more then but the singing voices. And now you are one of them.

The End

You stand still, as Mr. Spock has commanded. Spock begins to flicker in the spray of rainbow light, as in the ship's transporters. Then he fades away, and the light stops.

You go to the computer console, trying to figure out if it can tell you where Mr. Spock is and how to bring him back. Unfortunately, the displays and notes are all in Vulcan shorthand, which you cannot read.

After a while you figure out that the main control of the time-analyzer is a large lever on the computer console. But the notes do not tell you which way to move the lever.

If you push the lever forward, turn to page 61.

If you pull the lever back, turn to page 92.

You hold the lever steady. The clock whirls backward. Suddenly, the rainbow light pours across the room, and Mr. Spock walks backward out of it. The broken pieces of crystal jump off the floor and fit themselves together into a panel again.

Mr. Spock reaches past you and snaps the switch. The sound and light stop.

"Thank you, Ensign," he says. "I shall be much more careful . . . this time." He smiles at you. "Shall we go on with our experiments?"

The End

Mr. Spock tells you what channel you must use to contact your universe's *Enterprise* on subspace radio. You are to meet him in the Transporter room in half an hour.

You start toward the Bridge. In the corridors, crewmen are fighting with each other.

The Bridge doors open. "Well?" snarls the man in Captain Kirk's chair. You see that it *is* Captain Kirk, but he has knife scars on his face and hands, and you have never seen your Captain so angry.

"Replacement Communications Officer," you say, in the roughest voice you can manage.

"It's about *time* I got some time off," the mirror-Lieutenant Uhura grumbles, and shoves past you as she goes out the door.

You sit down at the console and begin sending code. Soon you receive an answering signal from the mirror-*Enterprise*. They will be ready to transport in exactly ten minutes, and you must be there or be left behind.

You feel Captain Kirk's hand grab your shoulder. "What are you doing?" he demands. "I didn't order any messages!"

If you shout back at him, trying to talk your way out of this, turn to page 97.

If you make a run for it, turn to page 100.

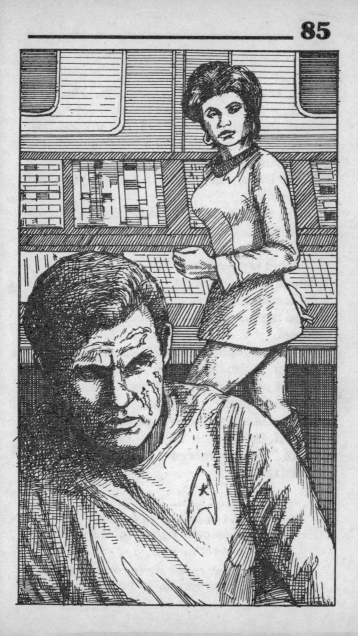

You reach for Mr. Spock's arm. The rainbow light falls across you as well.

You feel very dizzy, and for several moments you cannot see. Then your sight clears. You and Mr. Spock are standing in a ship's Science Laboratory—but not the one you were in before.

"You should not have done that, Ensign," Spock says, "but I thank you for trying to help."

"Where are we?" you ask.

Spock looks around. "This equipment is very familiar," he says. "I think we are still aboard the *Enterprise*—but about forty years in our past."

The door opens. Three Security men are standing there: They are wearing old-style Starfleet uniforms, very different from yours.

"Intruder alert!" one says.

Before Mr. Spock can explain, a guard says, "Careful, he's a Vulcan, they're stronger than we are." Another fires his phaser, and Mr. Spock falls.

If you think you had better surrender before things get any worse, turn to page 49.

If you run for it, turn to page 102.

PHASERS LOCKED ON, says your targeting computer. You squeeze the firing trigger.

A beam of blue light streaks toward the Klingon starship. It runs straight between the cruiser's engine pods, close enough to burn the surface but causing no real damage.

"Perfect, Ensign!" Captain Kirk says. "Lieutenant Uhura, open hailing frequencies to the Klingon vessel. Tell them to prepare to be boarded."

"Klingons don't surrender, Captain," Uhura says.

"I know that," says Kirk. Then he turns to you. "Have you ever led a boarding party, Ensign?"

"No, sir," you say.

"Now's your chance," says the Captain. "Get your gear and be at the Transporter room on the double."

Turn to page 66.

In the Starfleet Academy escape class, they told you that sometimes force fields can be shorted out with a piece of metal. You have a metal belt buckle that might work, but you also remember that it is a dangerous trick.

If you decide to wait and see what happens, turn to page 111.

If you try to short out the force field, turn to page 90.

"If time travel is possible," says Mr. Spock, "it may be possible to change the past. If my future self was right about this area of space having a twisted time-flow, we may be able to adjust the transporter to beam you back across time. Then you must try to prevent the time-field accident from ever happening."

Making the adjustments takes many days. Mr. Spock is quite calm as he works. You wonder if you could be as cool, if you had seen "yourself" die.

Finally, the transporter is ready. You step in. Mr. Spock says, "Good luck, Ensign," and pushes the controls.

You feel dizzy again, and cannot see for several seconds. Then you find yourself in the *Enterprise* Science Laboratory, where you started, the glowing crystal panels all around you. In front of you, you see Mr. Spock—and yourself! You realize that the accident will happen any second now.

If you call out for Mr. Spock to stop the experiment, go to page 103.

If you try to keep the crystal panel from breaking, turn to page 109.

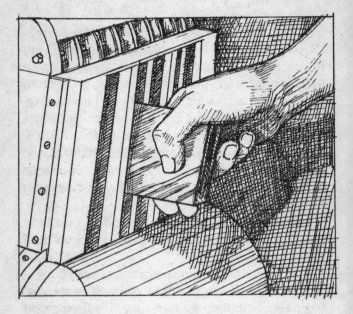

You take off your belt buckle, and bring it close to one of the metal plates that generate the force field. As you pry the buckle against the plate, there is a bright flash of energy.

You think that the flash is much too close for comfort. Then you think that this wasn't a very good idea.

That is the last thing you know.

The End

You go to the Bridge. The Captain turns as you enter. You remember from your Academy history lessons that he is Captain Robert April. "What is it, Ensign?" he says.

You explain who you are and how you came here with Mr. Spock. "Please believe me, Captain," you say.

"I believe you, Ensign," says Captain April. His voice is sad. "But you are too late. We had only a short time to send you back to your own time. Your Mr. Spock is already gone. He did not want to leave you, but there was no choice. This is your time now."

"Am I still an Ensign in Starfleet?" you ask.

"That I can arrange," Captain April says. "Welcome aboard the *Enterprise* . . . again."

You remember reading, at the Academy, about Captain April's adventures aboard the *Enterprise*. Now that you have changed the past, you wonder if those adventures will be yours as well.

The End

You pull back slowly on the lever. There is a noise like a strong wind, and the light in the laboratory turns a strange violet color. On the wall, the clock begins to run backward.

If you keep holding the lever back, turn to page 83.

If you let go of the lever, turn to page 94.

You concentrate, trying to block the Takoi thought signals out of your mind. The noise seems to get quieter. Dr. McCoy nods at you. "It's working," he shouts. "Keep at it, Ensign!"

You begin concentrating on the words to a Starfleet Academy song. Soon Kirk and McCoy are singing along with you, as loudly as they can. The Takoi seem to be confused by the noise. They start to move away from you and your stun beams.

As they do, Captain Kirk flips open his communicator. "Scotty! Three to beam up, fast!"

You and the officers flicker out, and reappear in the *Enterprise*'s Transporter room.

Dr. McCoy says, "Ensign, it was a good thing for us that you could resist the Takoi mind controls."

Kirk says, "Was that what saved us, Bones? I thought they were just trying to get away from our singing."

You all laugh, and walk out past a very puzzled transporter operator, singing.

The End

You let go of the time lever. The clock starts to count forward again, and the noises stop.

Then, without your willing it, your hand goes to the lever and pulls it again. Again the clock runs backward. Again you let go.

And again you pull the lever!

You are caught in a time loop, doomed to repeat the same five seconds over and over again, until . . .?

You wonder if Mr. Spock will be able to get you out of this.

Wherever, or whenever, Spock is . . .

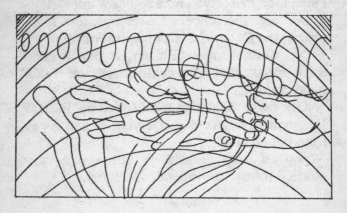

The End

"Sure," you say, and join the group guarding Mr. Spock.

You go to the ship's brig, and Spock is put in a prison cell. "Watch him while we get the Captain," a guard tells you. Then they leave you alone.

Quickly, you open the cell door and free Mr. Spock. "What's going on?" you ask.

"I believe we have traveled sideways in time," Spock says. "Captain Kirk and some of the other officers once visited an alternate universe, like a mirror image of ours. There the crew were all evil, violent versions of the people we know."

"How can we get home?" you ask.

"We must call our *Enterprise* on subspace radio, and then trade places with our mirrorselves through the transporter. That means we must each do a different task, and meet later."

If you want to send the subspace radio message, turn to page 84.

If you want to set the transporter, turn to page 99.

Drawing your knife, you slip quietly into the Transporter room, trying to sneak up behind the mirror-universe Black and Wu.

Swiftly, you jump on Black and knock him out with the handle of your knife. You turn to face Ensign Wu.

Unfortunately, this Ensign Wu is just as good a shot as the one in your universe.

You hope she is gone before Mr. Spock gets here. . . .

The End

"Why are you sending a message without my orders?" demands the mirror-world Captain Kirk.

"You *did* order it," you say, just as angrily. "What's the matter, can't you remember?" You hardly believe you are yelling at a starship captain.

The mirror-Kirk looks around. The other officers are waiting to see if he will admit he made a mistake.

He will not. "Of course I remember," he says, quickly covering up with a lie, "but it was a secret message. You should have sent it secretly. Now get out of here."

You are glad to obey that order. You leave the Bridge and go to the Transporter room, where you find Mr. Spock making adjustments to the controls.

"The message got through," you say.

"Excellent, Ensign," Spock says. "Now, timing is very important."

The two of you stand on the transporter platform. Rainbow light shimmers around you.

Go to page 116.

You pull out your knife and jump to attack the nearest guard. Mr. Spock kicks the gun out of another guard's hand. You reach Spock and cut the ropes tying his hands, and he uses Vulcan nerve pinches to knock out two more Security men. The last one runs away.

"What happened?" you ask. "Where are we?"

Spock says, "I believe we are in an alternate universe, one Captain Kirk once entered by accident. Here, the Federation is a vicious Empire. Everyone in our universe also exists here, but in an evil version."

You say, "How do we get home?"

"Since we are here, our mirror-selves must be in our universe. We must trade places through the transporter, and for that we must call *our Enterprise*. We will have to separate, and meet later."

Spock explains that there are two jobs to do: he will do one, and you will take the other.

If you want to send the message to the Enterprise in your universe. turn to page 84.

If you want to set the transporter to send you home, turn to page 99.

You make your way carefully to the Transporter room, avoiding the many arguments and fights you see in the hallways. The mirror-crew seem to do nothing but argue with each other.

Through the Transporter room door, you can see two Security Ensigns. You know them— that is, you know their mirror-selves: their names are Black and Wu. They both have phasers, while you have only a knife, and the two people you know are very good shots.

If you try to attack them anyway, hoping these two are not so good, turn to page 96.

If you try to trick Black and Wu into leaving the room, turn to page 101.

"Tell me what that message was!" the mirror-Kirk shouts, shaking you by the shoulder.

You kick him in the shins, pull away, and run for the door.

"Stop the spy!" says the Captain, and you hear phaser shots go past you. The door is just ahead. It opens.

Standing there are two Security guards, guns pointed at you.

As the mirror-crew close in on you, you hope that Mr. Spock gets home all right. . . .

The End

You walk casually into the Transporter room. "Hi, Black. Hello, Wu," you say, as if nothing is the matter.

"What do you want?" Black says.

"I just heard two Ensigns in the dining room say that you two couldn't hit the broadside of a Klingon cruiser," you say.

"What?" shouts Wu. "I'll give those two a good shooting lesson!"

"Wait," says Black. "We have to guard this room."

"I'll do that," you say.

"Good deal," says Wu, and they leave.

Quickly, you go to work, setting the transporter as Mr. Spock told you to do.

Soon Spock comes in. "The message is sent," he says. "We have no time to waste— Security is coming."

You hear shouts from the hallway as you and Spock stand on the transporter platform. Rainbow-colored light surrounds you. . . .

Go to page 116.

There is no way you can get out the door, with the Security men standing there. So you turn and run back into the laboratory, the guards' stun shots just missing you. You can hear alarms sound in the hallway outside.

While this ship is the U.S.S. *Enterprise*, it is almost completely different from the *Enterprise* you know. You have no idea where the doors and hallways might lead you.

But soon you must make a choice: Before you is a door out to the corridors, and a heavy metal door marked DANGER—NO ENTRY.

If you go out into the corridor, turn to page 110.

If you decide to risk the metal door, turn to page 108.

"Stop the experiment!" you shout. "The equipment is about to break down!"

Mr. Spock and "you" look up. It is very startling to see yourself across the room, and the other you is just as surprised.

Spock checks his instruments. "You are right," he says. "The Number Six panel was just about to shatter. But how did you know?"

"I . . . saw it happen," you say. Suddenly, you feel dizzy again. You look at your hands. You can see through them. You are vanishing!

Mr. Spock nods, seeming to understand. Then you understand too. Since you have stopped the time experiment, you will never travel in time. This "you" never existed. And now you are fading away, leaving behind the new, real "you."

The last thing you wonder is if that Ensign's adventures will be as strange as yours. . . .

The End

You grab your other self and hold on, as Mr. Spock steps off the transporter platform.

You feel very dizzy and weak. The other you walks right through your arms, as if you were a ghost, and turns to look at you.

Mr. Spock says, "You have changed the past, Ensign. Now there is only one future, only one you. The other one does not exist any more . . . but thank you, for what you did to save me."

"Good-bye," you hear yourself saying. You do not know which one of you spoke.

Then there is only one of you in the room.

The End

"One trip in time is enough for me," you tell Captain April. "I would rather stay here . . . if I could serve on the *Enterprise* with you, sir."

"I think that could be arranged," the Captain says. "What do you think, Mr. Spock?"

"Perhaps I can answer that, Captain," says the Mr. Spock from your own time. "Remember, this is happening forty years in my past. I recall the Ensign's coming aboard." Spock looks at you. "You will stay," he says.

"What will happen?" you ask the future Spock.

Turn to page 118.

"You will obey us," says the Takoi mind voice.

"Says who?" you think. "Captain Kirk! Dr. McCoy! Wake up!"

The Captain's eyes open. He looks around. In a moment he is on his feet, holding his phaser in one hand and shaking Dr. McCoy awake with the other.

You hear the Takoi voice saying, "The humans have resisted our control! We must subdue them again—all attack together!"

Again you hear the screaming sound of the aliens' mental attack. The Captain and Dr. McCoy are using their phasers to stun the Takoi, and the attack grows weaker each time an alien falls, but the two officers do not look as if they can last much longer.

"Ensign," says Captain Kirk, "can you do something?"

If you decide to fire your phaser at the ceiling of the room, turn to page 60.

If you want to try a mental counterattack, turn to page 93.

You pull open the heavy access door. It is very dark beyond, and there is a sound of machinery. You go through the door and close it behind you.

After a time, your eyes adjust to the dim light. You are inside the ship's computers; all around you are the circuit panels, alive with electricity, cooled by liquid helium at hundreds of degrees below zero. One false step here could be deadly!

If you go on through the computer area, turn to page 59.

If you decide to go back into the lab, hoping that the Security guards have gone, turn to page 112.

You move to the crystal panel that broke when you were here "before." Just as you reach it, however, it sparks and cracks apart. Light fills the room. "Do not touch me!" Mr. Spock says. You reach out and grab "yourself" by the sleeve, pulling the other "you" out of the time field.

The other Ensign turns around. You stare at one another for a while: It is a very strange feeling to look at yourself face to face.

Quickly, you explain to "yourself" what has happened.

"We haven't got any time to lose, then," the other says, and you both laugh at your own joke. Then, together, the two of you rush to the Transporter room.

Mr. Scott is very surprised to see identical twin Ensigns rush into the room. You explain to the Engineer how to adjust the transporter, as Mr. Spock on the long-ago *Enterprise* told you. Scott works fast.

A column of light appears on the platform. Mr. Spock is returning—very much alive!

Suddenly the other "you" says, "I think there's one too many of us here," and starts to jump up on the platform.

If you try to stop "yourself," turn to page 104.

If you do nothing, turn to page 113.

You go into the ship's hallways, being careful to stay out of sight. Soon you come to a turbo-elevator, and get in: "Crew's Quarters," you say. You do not know your way around this past-time version of the *Enterprise*, but the elevators will take you wherever you tell them to.

You go into one of the crew cabins and find an Ensign's uniform that fits you. Now you can move around the ship without being noticed.

If you go back to the Science Laboratory, and try to find a solution to your time problem, turn to page 114.

If you go to the Bridge, and try to explain your problem to the Captain, turn to page 91.

You wait, alone in your cell, for what seems like hours. Finally a group of officers appears. You do not know them, but you recognize the Captain's uniform.

"I am Captain Robert April of the U.S.S. *Enterprise*," he says. "Would you like to explain who you are?"

You remember reading about Captain April at the Academy. His adventures were very famous, but he died years before you were born, and you could never have hoped to meet him. Now you do your best to tell him who you are and how you got here.

The Captain says, "If you *are* a spy, you certainly chose a strange alibi. Mr. Spock, what do you think?"

Spock steps forward. Then you see he is much younger than the Spock you know. "We know time travel is possible, Captain. And I've just had a talk with someone who can only be my future self. We think we can reverse the time effect—but it will be very dangerous."

If you take the risk to return home, turn to page 114.

If you have had enough time-traveling, turn to page 105.

You wait for several minutes, then open the computer door and step back into the laboratory.

"Who are you?" you hear Mr. Spock's voice say. You see Spock, wearing one of the old *Enterprise* uniforms. Then you see that this Vulcan is many years younger than your Mr. Spock.

Quickly, you explain that you have accidentally traveled through time.

"I believe you," Spock says. "And I have seen the Vulcan who came with you: He indeed must be me. But I have some bad news for both of us. One of the Security guards did not set his phaser gun to STUN. Mr. Spock . . . *your* Mr. Spock, the one in my future . . . is dead."

You do not know what to say.

Spock says, "If we can travel into the past, perhaps we can change it as well. For both our sakes, I hope so. But I must ask you to do something very dangerous, and I cannot order you to do it."

If you agree to do what Spock has in mind, turn to page 89.

If you have taken enough risks already, turn to page 115.

The other "you" runs into the time field and vanishes. You start to follow.

"Wait, Ensign," Mr. Spock says. "There can be only one of you in any future. Your past self has gone through time to change the past in which I was killed . . . and, as you can see, you succeeded."

"How do you know you were killed?" you ask.

"Because you told me," Spock says. He points toward the empty time field. "That is, *that* version of you is going back now to tell me."

You say, "I'm a little bit confused."

Spock smiles. "So am I, Ensign. Experiments with time are like that. Now, I suggest that we go back to the laboratory and finish ours."

The End

You enter the laboratory. You are startled to see two Mr. Spocks standing there: the Spock from your time, and his own past self. They are working together on a piece of machinery with glowing crystal parts, similar to the one on the *Enterprise* you left.

"Come quickly, Ensign," the future-Spock says. "We have only a few minutes while the time field is open."

You, and your Mr. Spock, stand together in the rays of light from the rainbow crystals. "Good-bye," says the past-Spock. "It was fascinating to meet you . . . both of you."

You fade out in the colored light.

Turn to page 117.

You tell Mr. Spock that you are sorry, but you do not want to do any more time-traveling.

"I understand, Ensign," he says. "Perhaps we would only have made things worse."

In the time that follows, you are accepted into the Starfleet of your own past. After many years, you become Captain of a small ship on the Romulan border. Someday, your future self will graduate from the Starfleet Academy. You wonder if Mr. Spock will remember you, and be able to prevent the time accident.

You wonder if history *can* be changed.

But you may never know for certain.

The End

The transporter light disappears. You are still standing in the *Enterprise* Transporter room—but standing in front of you are the ship's officers, and they are smiling. The mirror-crew did not smile.

"Welcome back, Spock," Captain Kirk says. "I was interested to meet your mirror-self again, but I'm glad to have the real you aboard."

"Thank you, Captain," Spock says. "I could not have made it back without the Ensign's help."

"In that case," Kirk says, "I'm *very* glad to have you back, Ensign. Somebody has to get my officers out of the trouble they get into."

Mr. Spock smiles. Two others laugh at the Captain's joke. Soon you are laughing too . . . and you know that your adventure aboard the *Enterprise* has only just started.

The End

When you can see again, you are standing in the Science Laboratory of your *Enterprise,* the pieces of the crystal panel on the floor. Captain Kirk is there, looking at the broken crystal. Then he turns and sees you.

"There you are, Spock," he says. "Where have you been? I couldn't find you anywhere on the ship."

"The Ensign and I were doing an experiment," Spock says. "But we were on the *Enterprise* . . . all the time."

You and Mr. Spock exchange a secret smile.

The End

"You and Captain April will have many adventures together," Mr. Spock says. "If I said more . . . they would not be adventures. Now, I must return to my own time, before I make any changes in history."

The two Mr. Spocks, past and future, leave the room. Captain April looks at you and smiles.

"Welcome aboard, Ensign," he says. "Now come on. We've got a ship to run."

The End

NOW THAT YOU'VE COME TO THE END OF YOUR VERY OWN ADVENTURE DO YOU KNOW WHICH WAY TO GO FOR MORE?

Well, just try any or all of these thrilling, chilling adventure-on-every-page **WHICH WAY™** books!

- ___ #1 **THE CASTLE OF NO RETURN** 45756/$1.95
- ___ #2 **VAMPIRES, SPIES AND ALIEN BEINGS** 45758/$1.95
- ___ #3 **THE SPELL OF THE BLACK RAVEN** 45757/$1.95
- ___ #4 **FAMOUS AND RICH** 43920/$1.95
- ___ #5 **LOST IN A STRANGE LAND** 44110/$1.95
- ___ #6 **SUGARCANE ISLAND** 44189/$1.95
- ___ #7 **CURSE OF THE SUNKEN TREASURE** 45098/$1.95
- ___ #8 **COSMIC ENCOUNTERS** 45097/$1.95
- ___ #9 **CREATURES OF THE DARK** 46021/$1.95
- ___ #10 **INVASION OF THE BLACK SLIME AND OTHER TALES OF HORROR** 46020/$1.95
- ___ #11 **SPACE RAIDERS AND THE PLANET OF DOOM** 46732/$1.95
- ___ #12 **TRAPPED IN THE BLACK BOX** 46731/$1.95
- ___ #13 **STARSHIP WARRIOR** 50859/$1.95
- ___ #14 **POLTERGEISTS, GHOSTS AND PSYCHIC ENCOUNTERS** 46977/$1.95
- ___ #15 **STAR TREK: VOYAGE TO ADVENTURE** 50989/$1.95

POCKET BOOKS, Department AWW
1230 Avenue of the Americas, New York, N.Y. 10020

Please send me the books I have checked above. I am enclosing $_____ (please add 75¢ to cover postage and handling for each order, N.Y.S. and N.Y.C. residents please add appropriate sales tax). Send check or money order—no cash or C.O.D.s please. Allow up to six weeks for delivery. For purchases over $10.00, you may use VISA: card number, expiration date and customer signature must be included.

NAME_____

ADDRESS_____

CITY_____ STATE/ZIP_____

☐ Check here to receive your free Pocket Books order form.

913